TREASURE OF ICE AND FIRE

WAYNE D. DUNDEE

Based on a concept developed by David Cranmer
for the Veridical Dreams series, inspired by the
dreams journals of Kyle J. Knapp.

Cover image from Dreamstime.
Design by dMix.
Illustration of Kyle Knapp by Matt Tyszka.

ISBN: 978-1-943035-09-0

www.beattoapulp.com

Based
on the
dream
journals of
KYLE J. KNAPP

Praise for the work of WAYNE D. DUNDEE

"He has a knack for creating fully rounded characters, both heroes and villains."

—**James Reasoner**
Author of *Hunt at the Well of Eternity*

* * *

"Wayne Dundee keeps getting better with every book he puts out."

—**Peter Brandvold**
Author of the *Lou Prophet, Bounty Hunter* series

* * *

"Dundee doesn't write for the faint-hearted."

—**Mel Odom**
Author of *The Rover* series

CONTENTS

In another time ...

TREASURE OF ICE AND FIRE

PROLOGUE

Molak of the Wyvar regulators shivered inside his heavy cloak and cursed under his breath. The snow was coming down harder and the wind whipping into the maw of the mountain pass carried the ice-packed flakes with a viciousness that that made them sting like a thousand miniature daggers. On most occasions, Molak was proud to be a member of the regulators. But on a night like this he couldn't help thinking that there might be something to be said for having remained in the employ of his father, a liveryman by trade. The stables could be heavy with stench at times and could be stifling in the hot summer months, yet at least he never remembered a time when he felt like he was going to freeze to death.

Needing to move in order to keep some circulation flowing in his feet and legs, Molak walked over to a second man standing watch with him over the pass entrance. Evard was younger and more slightly built under his own heavy cloak and was clearly having a very hard time enduring these conditions.

"How are you holding up?" Molak said.

"Not very good," Evard replied in a weak voice. "I don't know how much longer I can stand it."

"You have to find a way. Walk around, stamp your

feet. You must manage to tough it out." Molak scowled in the direction of a nearby tent, a good-sized one made of thickly-layered animal hides that had been erected in a notch between two rock shoulders, out of the wind. Smoke that indicated a warm fire burning within lifted from an opening at the top of the tent only to be whisked away and dispersed. "If you go to the captain and tell him you can't stand your watch," Molak warned bitterly, "he will make it very hard on you."

"How can it be worse than this?" Evard pleaded.

"I don't know. But if anybody can find a way, he can."

A hint of irritation, maybe even anger, slipped into Evard's voice and made it stronger. "It might not be so bad if this made any sense. But there's no way that rogue priest Nindocai is on the move on a night like this. From all reports, he's a frail old man. No matter how badly he wants to slip away from the lowlands where they monitor him too closely, he wouldn't be risking his life to try it in these conditions."

"I don't know about that. But what I do know," Molak said stubbornly, "is what a bad idea it would be for you to go to the captain and tell him ..."

He abruptly let his words trail off, pausing to concentrate more keenly on a foreign sound that had managed to slip through the howling night and reach his ears. There it was again ... the creak of a wheel ... the chuff of a laboring horse.

"What is it?" Evard wanted to know.

Molak pointed to the murky shapes approaching their position. "There. Someone is coming."

In short order, a heavy wagon covered by a wind-battered canvas canopy emerged out of the driving snow and reached the two guards. The wagon was drawn by two sturdy horses and two men, also sturdy-looking, sat on the open front seat. Both were wrapped in thick cloaks with fur hats pulled down tight on their heads. Additionally, each had a wrap of burlap covering the lower half of his face.

At the sight of the facial covering, which comprised a mask of sorts, both Molak and Evard became more sharply alert and extended their long spears toward the wagon and its occupants.

"Halt, and state your business!" ordered Molak.

The driver of the team complied, pulling back on the reins and bringing the snow-flecked horses to a stop.

"We are from the village of Felnar below," stated the driver, pulling down the covering over his mouth, "We are on a medical mission, bound for the valley of Gahm."

"What sort of medical mission?" Molak wanted to know.

"We have a very sick youth in back," explained the driver. "The physicians do not give him much chance to survive. We are his cousins. It has fallen to us to return the lad to his home village, to his mother and siblings, for what likely will be his final hours."

"What manner of illness does he suffer?"

The two men on the wagon seat exchanged uncertain looks. Finally, the second man turned back to Molak and said, "It is a fever of some sort. The physicians have bled him and treated him thoroughly, but cannot break it. Thus the conclusion that it likely will be fatal and it is best to return the patient to his closest kin."

"We will have to have a look at him," said Evard.

Another exchange of looks between the men on the wagon. Then: "Very well. Come around to the back, we have a lantern inside that we can light out of the wind."

The four moved around to the rear of the wagon. A canvas flap on the back end of the canopy was pulled back and flint was struck to a lantern hanging within. A flickering pool of light poured from the lantern and illuminated a still, blanket-covered form lying atop a straw mat on the floor of the wagon bed. The latter also contained a handful of wooden crates and a couple stout barrels that were pushed to either side and lashed in place.

"Pull back the blankets so we can have a proper look at the lad," instructed Molak.

"Is that really necessary?" questioned one of the cousins. "He's ill enough, must we expose him further to this night's harsh conditions?"

"You heard me. Pull back those blankets," Molak insisted.

Grudgingly, the order was obeyed. And when the innermost fold of the blanket was lifted, the pale, handsome face of a young man was revealed ... as well as the bright red spots that dotted its smooth features.

Molak and Evard fairly leaped backward, slipping and stumbling slightly to maintain their footing in the deepening snow. "The boy is poxed!" Evard wailed.

"That is why you have the covering over your

treacherous faces," accused Molak. "You knew all along you were carrying contaminated cargo!"

"No, no," protested one of the wagoneers. "He did not exhibit those spots before. The fever must have brought them out!"

Molak brandished his spear. "You lie! I ought to run you through."

"Do that," said the other man from the wagon, "it will be up to you to deal with the boy and his ailment."

"Leave them go," urged Evard. "Hasten them on their way, in fact! The sooner they are gone from here, the less chance for that cursed pox to spread."

Molak was quick to see the logic in his comrade's words. "You're right," he agreed. Then he once more thrust his spear menacingly toward the wagoneers. "You heard him. Snuff that lantern and close that wagon back up tightly. Be quick about it! Then get on with you. The sooner the better, you disease peddlers. And if you live to come down off that mountain in the spring, you'd better make sure I never see either of your ugly faces again—if I do, I'll slice them off below the chin with the point of my spear!"

* * *

Well beyond the guard post, over the crown of the pass, the wagon pulled once more to a halt. The men in front twisted around on their seat, pulled back a canvas flap, and the driver called into the cargo area, "It is safe now. Light the lantern again and roust yourselves. We have only a short way to go before we'll be able to find better shelter."

Activity stirred in the dark recess of the wagon bed before the lantern flared once more. When it did, it showed the "poxed" youth having risen to his knees amidst the blankets formerly swathed about him and setting the light to higher illumination. His movements appeared quite strong and nimble, hardly those of one deemed to be mortally ill. As the young man adjusted the lantern, a lid on one of the stout barrels abruptly wobbled and seemed to lift itself. After it had fallen away completely, a shape formerly crouched and tucked inside the vessel rose up rather stiffly to a standing position, revealing itself to be a tall, thin man of advanced years.

The boy quickly turned and reached to aid the oldster in climbing the rest of the way free from the confines of the barrel. A wide smile spread across the younger man's face. "Your ruse worked perfectly, Master Nindocai. They practically offered to shovel a path in order to move us more quickly on our way."

One of the wagoneers up front chuckled heartily. "That they did. They couldn't get rid of us and our 'cousin' soon enough."

Now it was the old man's turn to smile as he reached out and wiped away some of the berry juice spots that he had earlier applied to the youth's face. "Yes, I had little doubt that they would react in such a way once they laid eyes on these," he said. Then, pressing both hands to the small of his back and stretching to work out some of the kinks brought on by being confined inside the barrel, he added, "The next time I serve up such a plot, however, I assure one and all that, if I play another part in it, it will include a far lesser degree of discomfort for myself."

"We'll work on offsetting that just as soon as we can," the wagon driver told him. "I know this pass well, even in a storm like this. Not too far ahead there will be a break off to our right, a long crevice almost like a narrow canyon. It will buffer us well from the wind. We can build a fire and finish the night in far greater comfort."

"The storm should break by morning," predicted the second wagoner. "If we get a good, clear start we will be well into the valley of Gahm by tomorrow evening. There is an out-of-the-way little inn there where we can revive ourselves all the better and from there plot the rest of our journey."

Nindocai nodded. "Aye. The journey. And a long, arduous one it remains. But we have completed an important early hurtle so we must take heart. Lead on, hail fellows. A small slice of improved comfort for the balance of this night sounds like a wonderful next step."

I

When Nindocai was drawn from his slumber in the middle of the night and first heard the faint, distant ringing of the hammer, he knew it must be another sign—a message of some kind—from the goddess Arya. That it implied a link to the "secret hammer" part of what she had previously imparted, there seemed little doubt. Still, the holy man couldn't help being reluctant to immediately react. Not at this hour, not on this bitter cold night. He tried convincing himself it might be better to ponder he matter further from the warmth of his bed and then be able to arrive at a more certain interpretation in the morning.

But it was in vain.

The hammer kept ringing, steel on steel.

And sleep could not be re-captured by the old man.

Finally, Nindocai sat up in his blankets, feeling annoyed but fighting to suppress the emotion. Arya seemed to be growing more demanding with what she expected from him and less patient for him to take action ... never mind that he often failed to understand fully what it was she wanted, at least not at first. Yet dragging one's feet when it came to responding to the wishes of a goddess (even one diminished in both power and a following these days) hardly seemed like a good idea.

Nindocai did not want to leave his blankets. It was cold in the room and would be far more so outside. But apparently that's where he'd be venturing. The hammer continued to ring and, whatever else it might mean, the demand for him to go investigate could not be ignored.

By the faint illumination cast under the room's single door from the great stone fireplace out in the common area of the remote inn, Nindocai began pulling on his clothes. He dressed quietly so as not to disturb Ryle, who lay peacefully asleep on the straw pallet over against the wall. After pulling on his fur-lined boots, the oldster paused momentarily, second-guessing himself to wonder if perhaps he *should* wake the lad. But no, he decided with finality, there was no need for that. Not until he'd had his chance to do some investigating.

Out in the common area, the warmth from the crackling fireplace was most welcome. Nindocai stood before it for a long moment, the dancing flames making shifting patterns of light across the dome of his shaven head and the thin wisps of gray beard that trailed down around his mouth and off his chin. He willed the heat to soak deep into the bones of his gaunt frame, knowing it would be leaving him quickly enough once he stepped outside.

He couldn't tell exactly what time it was, only that it was somewhere in the wee hours of the morning. A quick peek through a crack in one of the shuttered windows had shown a cold, clear sky—still full dark save for a sprinkling of ice chip stars, with no hint of dawn's glow anywhere along the rim of the horizon.

Somewhere in the distance, the hammer continued to ring in the performance of its task. Nindocai found this somewhat puzzling, in that the task of waking him and gaining his attention had already been accomplished. In addition to being generally vague, the messages from Arya were also usually quite terse. If the sound of the hammer came at her bidding, it was dragging on well beyond the norm.

"Can I be of some assistance, sir?"

The voice, though soft and meek, startled Nindocai. Turning sharply, he saw that the inquiry had come from Sandor, the inn's slight, copper-haired servant boy, who now stood at his elbow, peering attentively up at him.

"Critt's Thunder, boy! You gave me a start."

"I did not mean to. My sincere apologies, sir," Sandor said earnestly.

"Where did you come from, anyway? And why are you prowling about at such an hour?"

Sandor pointed past a corner of the fireplace. "In cold weather, my sleeping pallet is kept back there. It is my job to get up as necessary during the night to make sure the fire is kept stoked so that the common area is always warm for the comfort of our guests ... Hearing you leave your room caused me to wonder if you were feeling ill or perhaps seeking some refreshment from the kitchen. Either way, I thought I might be of some help."

Nindocai cleared his throat, feeling properly chagrined. "That was very kind of you, lad. Please excuse my gruff tone. When you reach such an advanced age as mine, you sometimes startle too easily.

13

And, alas, sometimes you also do not sleep as deeply as you might wish."

"Was it the sound of the hammer that woke you?" Sandor asked.

This gave Nindocai another, albeit milder, start. Usually when Arya sent him a message, only his eyes or ears were able to discern it. Such had been the case with the prophecy that brought about him and Ryle's journey to this remote valley in the first place. But now this. If the distant ringing of the hammer was indeed a signal from Arya, then Nindocai would have expected it to be audible only to him.

"Yes," the old man said in answer to the boy's query. "I was ... curious about the sound of that hammer at such a late—or early, depending on how one looks at it—hour."

"Most nights," Sandor answered, "the mists and heavy fog that settles over our valley muffles the sound so that it doesn't disturb our guests. On the rare occasions when it does, we are to explain that it is miners working deep in the earth high up on the mountain."

Nindocai frowned. "You say that with very cautious phrasing ... 'we are to explain' ... as if it might be a well-scripted answer rather than a factual one."

The boy did not wither under the elder's frown. Instead he met Nindocai's penetrating gaze with a mixed expression of boldness and curiosity. "Master Ersk said the he could tell right off that you were a man of great wisdom and a higher purpose than others who travel here to the valley of Gahm. Perhaps a priest of the old gods, he speculated. He was excited but at the same time nervous. He senses your presence here signals something very important for our little valley, perhaps all of Brassik ... Yet he is anxious about the role he might be called upon to play as a result."

Nindocai's expression turned thoughtful. "Your master sounds like a man with more insight than the unsuspecting might ascribe to a simple inn keeper. And you, boy, are quite sharp and attentive in your own way."

"*Are* you a priest of the old gods?"

"What if I am? Have the people of this valley—like so many once brave and pious citizens down on the plains and in the lowland cities—turned their backs on the old gods out of fear instilled by oppression from the godless Wyvar hordes who have invaded and taken over our country?"

Sandor set his jaw firmly, considering hard, before answering. Then: "Though it is done with great caution due to spies and the roaming bands of Wyvar regulators, I believe that the worship and belief in all powerful Critt and his family of gods and goddesses is as strong as ever here in this valley. In fact, the source of that hammering you hear lies in the ruins of a temple once dedicated to Arya, the Goddess of Hope. A secret chamber deep within the ruins still serves, among other purposes, as a place of worship."

Nindocai's eyes shone bright. "A temple to Arya with at least a portion still standing? I haven't seen or heard of such in years! Down in the lowlands, all the old temples have been flattened by the Wyvar curs to nothing but pebbles and dust … You must tell me. How do I get to these temple remains?"

This time Sandor did not hesitate. He smiled and said, "I can do better than tell you, sir. Allow me to show you."

* * *

From his lookout post up on the high, cold ledge, Spreek the Scrounger came scrambling down into the sunken chamber aglow with light and heat from the bellows-amplified forge coals. With surprising speed, given his twisted form and spider-like limbs and the tortured manner in which this forced him to move, he scuttled across the stone floor and drew close to the tall, powerfully built man standing before the forge.

"Someone is coming. Visitors approach," Spreek announced.

The tall man paused with his massive steel hammer poised to strike down on the glowing object held in the strong grip of tongs across the working surface of an anvil. Scowling, he turned his broad, sweat-beaded face to Spreek. "Regulators?"

"No," the misshapen scrounger replied. "There are but two of them. One is quite small, the other is tall but frail-looking. The latter I do not recognize, but he walks slowly and cautiously over the rocky path, like a man of advanced years. The small one, I believe, is the servant boy from the Boar's Tusk Inn.

"Sandor," said the tall man, indicating a familiarity with the inn servant. "He can be trusted not to bring anyone here who might mean us harm."

"*If* his judgment is sound. He is but a boy, after all. And quite an impertinent one, if you ask me. I don't know that I would put too much faith in him."

"I would." The tall man's statement was firm. "Go meet them, escort them down."

"If you say so." Spreek did little to hide his disapproval. His expression brightened a moment later, however, as he thought of something. "Once I've brought them down, I probably should also remain. In case of trouble." *And where it is far warmer than my freezing lookout perch*, he thought to himself.

The tall man smiled tolerantly. "I think I can probably handle any trouble from a boy and an old man," he said. "Best you return to your lookout post, in case there *is* some trickery afoot and the pair has been followed."

Again making no attempt to hide the disappointment now combined with his disapproval, Spreek scuttled off. Once he had gone, the tall man put aside that which he had been working on and walked over to where a water bucket hung suspended in a shadowy corner of the chamber. He carried the hammer with him. With his free hand, he scooped a gourd of cool water from the bucket and drank deeply. A second gourdful of water he poured over his head and upturned face. With a towel snatched from where it hung on a nearby nail, he wiped the excess from his face and neck.

Spreek returned with the visitors.

Nindocai edged immediately to stand close to the forge, welcoming its warmth after the bitter trek from the inn. He extended his long-fingered, heavily veined hands from under his heavy cloak and rubbed them briskly together.

"Welcome to my fire," said the tall man, emerging from the shadows. "I'm afraid that its heat and perhaps a drink of cool water are all that I can offer in the way of hospitality."

Nindocai turned his head, continuing to rub his hands together as he held them out toward the glowing coals. "Your heat I accept with great appreciation," he said. Then, smiling, he added, "At the moment, however, I find no appeal in the thought of a cool drink."

"Understandable. It is a bitter night out there. Working down here at the forge, I sometimes tend to forget that."

"In case you need reminding," Spreek interjected, "neither is my lookout post exactly warm and cozy."

Again the tall man smiled tolerantly. "Ah, but in the summer months, when the valley is oppressively hot, your perch is very cool and comfortable, is it not? Therefore, you have balance in your life. You should consider that a blessing … Now scoot on back to your post. Dawn isn't that far away and with it will come breakfast including plenty of hot tea to warm you."

Spreek turned to shuffle away, muttering, "Very well … I just hope it's not too late and I am nothing but a frozen carcass unable to ingest any saving nourishment."

Once the reluctant lookout had departed, the tall man turned back to Nindocai. "I trust young Sandor here did the necessary introductions between you and

Spreek," he said as he shifted his hammer to his left hand and extended his right. "I am called Daer."

"And I am Nindocai," said the elder, taking the extended hand rather cautiously, somewhat fearful that his might be crushed in a powerful grip. In spite of the unmistakable strength behind it, however, the grip was controlled and actually quite gentle.

Withdrawing his hand, Nindocai used it to make a sweeping gesture that indicated the chamber and the ruins all about it, saying, "Sandor tells me that this used to be a temple to the goddess Arya."

"As far as most of us here in the valley of Gahm are concerned," Daer replied rather sternly, "it still is. The Wyvar dogs may have pulled down much of the manmade structure, but the spirit of the goddess—and all the rest of the old gods overseen by Almighty Critt—can still be found here by those who remain willing to believe and worship."

Nindocai regarded him intently. "Spoken boldly and bravely, my son."

Sandor, who had been standing by in respectful silence, now spoke up. "Daer is the bravest man in all the valley—probably all of Brassik!"

Daer smiled down at the boy. "What have I told you about speaking too freely, young one, and especially about holding me up as some kind of hero? There are countless men fighting in Brassik's freedom army, putting their lives on the line to try and drive out the Wyvar invaders, who daily exhibit far greater bravery than mine."

"But you risk your life too," the boy protested.

"Night after night, whenever the silencing fog is thick enough to mute your work from the regulator patrols, you forge weapons for the freedom army to fight with. Without your blades, their chances for success would be greatly reduced."

"Is it true?" said Nindocai, pressing Daer as he continued to regard him closely. "I've heard stories of the mysterious armorer who furnishes the freedom army with the finest weapons that any fighting man has ever taken into combat."

Daer shrugged his broad shoulders. "That is not for me to say. I am but a common blacksmith who takes pride in his work and does the best he can with all that he produces. Every spare piece of scrap I can get my hands on—and here I must also credit Spreek who, in addition to providing lookout services, is the most gifted of scroungers—I melt down and turn into weapons for the freedom fighters." Another shrug. "It is the least I can do."

"Yes. Yes, I see it now. More and more pieces falling into place to make the picture clearer," said Nindocai thoughtfully. He gestured to Daer's hammer. "And to do your crucial yet secretive work, you require a critical tool. A secret hammer."

Daer frowned. "No blacksmith accomplishes much without a good hammer. That is hardly a secret."

"But the work you do with it, at least insofar as the weapons you make for the freedom army," Nindocai insisted, "*that* is a secret. Is it not?"

"From the Wyvar regulators, yes." Daer paused, appraising the man before him more cautiously, perhaps even with a hint of suspicion. Then he said, "I welcomed you here and have spoken freely out of respect for Sandor's judgment in bringing you to this place. Now I feel it is time for you to be a bit more forthcoming about who you are and what end you pursue."

Nindocai tipped his head in a faint nod. "Very well. That is reasonable. Allow me to show you two items that will, I believe, go a long way toward explaining the circumstances for my being here."

So saying, the elder turned and walked over to a rough wooden work bench that stood in better light cast from the forge. Daer and Sandor followed, the blacksmith continuing to carry his massive hammer.

After removing his heavy outer cloak, Nindocai reached inside the collar of his tunic and withdrew a talisman strung on a silver chain. He held this out, letting it rest in the palm of his hand. It was the symbol for Arya, the Goddess of Hope. Upon seeing it, both Daer and Sandor automatically made signs of devotion to the goddess, touching the tips of their thumbs first to their foreheads for Belief and then to their hearts for Hope.

Nindocai paused, smiling, before he said, "For starters, I hope you will accept this as evidence that I am a priest of the old gods, dedicated to the sect of Arya."

"I knew it! Master Ersk guessed as much," Sandor whispered excitedly.

"Sadly, I can only reveal this fact with considerable discretion. Any recognition or open worship of the old gods, as you of course know, is strictly forbidden throughout Brassik since the overthrow by the Wyvar horde. That is why this" —again Nindocai made a gesture to indicate their surroundings— "even these crumbled ruins are such a rare treat to my eyes. Where I come from, I give counsel and hold services wherever and whenever I can gather a flock safely away from the ever vigilant eyes of the regulators or sniveling spies. But to once again hold a service in an actual temple, damaged though it may be, would bring great personal joy."

"Maybe before you leave our valley, that could be arranged," Sandor suggested eagerly.

"Perhaps," said Nindocai, a wistfulness in his tone. Then, more sternly, he added, "But a matter far more pressing than the faded desires of an old holy man is at stake. That is the real crux of why I am here."

From the folds of his clothing he took a second item, a parchment, which he spread out on the surface of the work bench. "Half a moon cycle ago," Nindocai said somberly, "the goddess Arya spoke to me in the middle of the night. She frequently contacts me with signs and messages, usually in more obscure ways. But on this occasion—and for two consecutive nights at exactly the same hour—it was her own sweet, pure voice speaking to me." He tapped the parchment with a slender finger. "What I have recorded here were her words."

Daer and Sandor leaned forward with great reverence and read:

To sever the bonds of oppression

The pure-hearted serpent
Must join with the secret hammer
In the ice-shrouded North
To secure the treasure of the frozen fire beast
And provision the freedom army

After studying the parchment for a long moment, Sandor lifted his eyes and said in an awed yet uncertain tone, "But what does it mean?"

Nindocai smiled. "To be honest, I am not completely sure. As I said earlier, the messages I get from the goddess are usually somewhat obscure. Nevertheless, I have in the past always managed to interpret them. As I will this one … Part of it I knew before coming here. And now I believe I have just solved another piece of the, er, puzzle." With that, the holy man tipped his head and let his gaze touch meaningfully on the heavy tool still held by the blacksmith.

In an excited gush, Sandor said, "Daer and his hammer—*the secret hammer!*"

Daer's mouth turned down at the corners and he was quick to protest. "Here now!"

"I believe the boy is exactly right," Nindocai said firmly.

"How can it be? I know nothing of frozen fire beasts and surely you can see I am hardly a man with any wealth or treasure at his disposal. I am a simple blacksmith barely eking out a living. And I already do all that I can to provision the freedom army."

"Precisely. Yet you do so *in secret*," Nindocai

insisted, "with the use of *a hammer* as your primary tool … It provides an answer too well suited to an interpretation of Arya's words. What else could have led me to this remote valley and then revealed to me these features that so closely match?"

"What about the rest of her words?" Daer wanted to know. "Have you matched anything else to them? If not, then me and my hammer don't really gain you much, do we? So how about you just leave us out of it and be on your way … If and when you figure out the other pieces to your puzzle, come back around again and maybe we'll be more interested."

"Ah, but I already have made another key match to Arya's message," Nindocai was quick to respond. "And I will further point out that we are well up into Brassik's 'ice-shrouded North' in contrast to the lowlands from whence my small party and I started."

Scowling, Daer said, "That is all well and good. But let *me* point that the ice-shrouded North covers quite a large territory, much of which still sprawls ahead of us. It strikes me that a truly *key match* to your message would be some more specific indicator of where the treasure can be found. Or even some clear idea of what the 'frozen fire beast' is supposed to mean. To the best of my knowledge, mythological creatures are mighty scarce these days … Do you have an answer for either of those things?"

"No," said Nindocai, starting to show annoyance. "But the interpretations to Arya's message seem to be coming in sequence. You and your hammer, I maintain, cover the second critical part. I agree that the need to venture deeper into the frozen lands will still lie before us. By so proceeding, I believe that—"

"Wait a minute," Daer interrupted. "Are you saying that you've already accounted for 'the pure-hearted serpent'?"

Sandor's eyes went wide as he asked excitedly, "You have a serpent with you back at the Boar's Tusk Inn?"

Seeing that the tone of his audience, particularly where Daer was concerned, had once again grown more curious than suspicious, Nindocai chose his words carefully. "Yes, it is true that I brought with me the match for Arya's 'pure-hearted serpent' requirement." He paused to fix his gaze imploringly on Daer. "I know that the work you are doing here, sir, is vitally important. But if you can bring yourself to only briefly trust me—if not as a devout holy man then merely as a fellow worshiper of the goddess Arya—I can reveal to you more evidence back at the inn that I believe will increase your belief in my claims and show that a matter of even greater importance is at hand … And *you* are fated to be a crucial part of what is to come."

II

By now, Ryle told himself, he should be used to showing his unusual birthmark to people. But after keeping it concealed for so many years out of fear it might be taken as some sort of demonic mark or bad omen, being requested to reveal it so often of late—especially to complete strangers—was awkward and a little embarrassing, to say the least. Offsetting these personal apprehensions, however, was the recent revelation that the mark meant something important. Something that could be very beneficial to the freedom army in which Ryle's older brother, Aron, held a high rank. Therefore, if Aron could endure the hardships and danger that came with battling the hated Wyvar invaders, then the least Ryle could do was suffer a bit of embarrassment if it would somehow be helpful to the cause.

So when Nindocai rousted him from his sleeping pallet and implored him to come meet some people who would be joining them in their quest, Ryle knew it would once again mean displaying his birthmark. Nevertheless, he dutifully rose, dressed, and then emerged out into the inn's common area from the room he and the holy man had shared for the night. Through a window where one of the shutters had been folded back, the lad could see that it was growing light with the onset of dawn. From back in the kitchen area came the clank of pots and pans, signaling that the inn keeper and his wife were beginning to prepare breakfast.

As he edged over to absorb some heat from the great fireplace, Ryle was somewhat surprised to see that the inn's servant boy was standing idly next to Nindocai and not busy with his share of the noisy kitchen activities. (He would learn later that Nindocai had compensated the inn keeper, Ersk, for an exclusive though temporary claim to the boy's time.) Standing with the holy man as well, evidently also rousted by him from their own room, were Grist and Lodor, two men from the freedom army that Aron had assigned to accompany and protect Nindocai and Ryle on their quest. Lastly, two additional men whom Ryle had never seen before also stood as part of the group that appeared to be awaiting him.

Large and intimidating as Grist and Lodor were (the exact reasons they'd been chosen for this assignment), one of the strangers was taller, broader, and equally imposing. The latter he accomplished even though he carried—in contrast to the swords and close-quarter combat spears the protectors were armed with—only a heavy workman's hammer slipped through his belt. The second stranger made an even sharper contrast, being small and deformed and looking quite overwhelmed by the towering men on all sides of him.

But it was the tall stranger's hammer that riveted Ryle's attention. It took a moment for the possible significance of the tool to fully register. When it did, a surge of excitement coursed through the lad and drew from him an openly intense appraisal of the stranger in possession of it.

Seeing this, the corners of Nindocai's mouth lifted the way they sometimes did with a hint of vague wisdom known only to him. "Yes, Ryle," he said, "what I recognize you taking note of is, I believe, an important development in the success of our mission."

"The secret hammer?" Ryle asked.

Nindocai nodded. "Indeed. That is my opinion."

"Although one not universally accepted," grumbled Daer.

"Do you recall," Nindocai went on, side-stepping the blacksmith's remark and focusing on Ryle, "hearing tales about a mysterious armorer who discreetly makes weapons of the finest quality for our freedom fighters?"

Before Ryle could answer, Lodor interjected. "Aye, I have heard such tales and I can vouch first hand as to the proclaimed quality. Woe that we don't have hundreds more of those fine weapons reaching the hands of our men, that's the only problem."

"I second that," agree Grist, bobbing his head eagerly.

Accepting these statements as sufficient responses to his question, Nindocai swept one arm in a gesture to indicate Daer, whose expression showed a troubled mix of being pleased by the praise for his weapon-making skills yet still half-scowling over the way he was being painted as someone destined to be part of a quest fostered by some murky dream. "I give you Daer," Nindocai announced to Ryle, "the man—the *craftsman*—responsible for the weapons of which we speak. At considerable risk from the prowling regulator patrols, from whatever scrap metal he can scrounge, he hammers out blades and axes and spear heads in the late hours on nights whenever the fog and mists are thick enough to muffle his work."

"The secret hammer. It *does* fit," said Ryle in an awed tone.

"We've already covered that—as a *possibility*," Daer reminded Nindocai. "We didn't interrupt my weapon-making and come here to belabor that point any further. We came here because you said you could show me additional evidence to match what you call your message from the goddess Arya."

"As I shall," Nindocai assured him. "I've already introduced you to Grist and Lodor, our protectors as assigned by Commander Aron of the freedom army. That, in itself, should carry some weight—the fact that such a highly regarded officer in the cause of liberating Brassik believes in our quest … To add to that, allow me to now introduce you to Ryle" —as he said this, the holy man placed a hand on the lad's shoulder— "youngest brother to Commander Aron."

Daer and Ryle exchanged nods of acknowledgement.

"And, if it matters to anybody, I am Spreek," said the deformed little man.

"Without Spreek's skill at supplying material," Nindocai explained, "Daer's output of much-needed weaponry would be seriously curbed."

"To be sure," Daer confirmed.

Then, getting back to the matter of providing the blacksmith with additional evidence to help convince him that the overriding matter at hand had validity, Nindocai continued, "Shortly after Ryle here was born, his parents sent for me and showed me that which we are about to show you. They feared it was a demon stamp, an omen possibly dooming the infant to some ghastly fate. In the end, after some pondering and prayerful reflection, I was able to convince them it was nothing but a curious yet benign birthmark. However, to avoid the poisonous tongues and trouble-making ways of those certain to be superstitious and spiteful if the mark were openly displayed, it was agreed from that early stage to keep it covered and maintained as a secret known only to the family ... Until now. Until the message from Arya gave it a meaning and purpose that could no longer be kept hidden ... Show him, lad."

Anticipating what was going to be asked of him, Ryle had already loosened the laces of the leather cuff always worn to cover his right wrist and forearm. Spreading the cuff open wider, the blond-haired youth now slipped it free. Revealed on the underside of his arm, a rose-hued natural imprint into his otherwise pale flesh, was the unmistakable shape of a wriggling serpent complete with a wedge-shaped head pointing toward the base of his palm.

"Critt's Thunder!" exclaimed Daer.

Grist and Lodor, who'd been privy to seeing the mark before, nonetheless could not maintain impassive expressions upon viewing it once again. And neither Sandor nor Spreek could keep their mouths from gaping wide as they looked on.

"Do you see? What could be more pure of heart than an infant, the bearer of this when first I saw it?" asked Nindocai rhetorically. "And, although I had scarcely thought about the child with the unfortunate birthmark in the intervening years, as soon as I heard Arya's phrase 'the pure-hearted serpent' I knew what it meant. It meant that young Ryle here was the first piece of the goddess's puzzle that, once completed, may mean the liberation of Brassik ... And you, reluctant Daer, I continue to believe with all my might represent the second phrase, 'the secret hammer'."

For the first time, the expression on Daer's broad face conveyed a wavering of his refusal to accept the holy man's interpretation. But, before the blacksmith could say anything, Ersk, the corpulent inn keeper, came waddling from the kitchen carrying a pot of tea on a tray also containing an array of stone cups. As the host leaned to place his tray atop the table around which the group was gathered, his gaze fell on Ryle's exposed arm and its distinctive stamp.

The inn keeper seemed to take the sight in stride, saying calmly, "Now there's something you don't see every day. What an unusual tattoo. Especially on a lad of such tender years."

"That's not a tattoo," Sandor was quick to correct him. "It's a birthmark."

This elicited a somewhat stronger reaction. "Dare say you! Well then. All the more unusual, says I. And such a near perfect replication it is."

"Yes, we are aware that it looks uncommonly like a

serpent," allowed Nindocai.

"True. But I was thinking of something else, something quite apart from that. The pattern of curves and twists, the triangular widening where a head might be—to me, I see it more as an uncannily close match to the odd-shaped body of water that lies in the mountains farther north. Serpentine Lake, the locals call it. I thought the lad might be from that region, hence my guess the mark was perhaps a tattoo representing such."

"A lake farther north, you say?" The edge of fresh excitement creeping into Nindocai's tone was unmistakable.

"That's right. It is a remote, seldom-visited place. Frozen over all but a few weeks each year. And even that small amount of thaw is only at the near end, the tail of the serpent if you will. At the far end, where the lake flares out into the wedge shape that resembles a head, it butts up against a perpetual wall of ice known to the locals, for whatever obscure reason, as *the Dragon Glacier*."

* * *

No sooner had Nindocai and his group—expanded now by Daer, Spreek, and Sandor—departed from the Boar's Tusk Inn, than its proprietor found himself enmeshed in the unfortunately familiar activity of arguing with his shrewish wife, Gretchel.

"For the life of me," she scolded, "I cannot fathom what you use for a brain sometimes. Aiding and abetting that band of rabble who are so openly aligned with the rebel forces continuing their futile resistance to our Wyvar rulers. The battle for Brassik is over. We lost. The sooner everybody accepts that, the sooner we can all start to benefit from more peaceful and prosperous conditions."

"The only peace will be the kind that comes from cowering at the feet of conquering dogs," Ersk maintained. "And only the regulator lords who levy tax after tax on those of us who once called ourselves proud Brassikans will ever know true prosperity. They will make certain of that, just like they've been doing ever since the overthrow."

"We still have our inn, do we not?" Gretchel insisted.

"With which we are barely managing to get by."

"And was it any different before? We are a remote inn in a rugged location with harsh weather conditions much of the year. If you wanted prosperity and security, my stubborn husband, you might have taken those things into consideration when you persisted in buying this place. I tried to tell you then, but you refused to listen."

"Yes, you tried to tell me," Ernst admitted with a ragged, weary sigh. "And you have continued telling me—over and over and over again—practically every day of our lives since."

"Then let me tell you something more," Gretchel replied harshly. "If you want the regulators to clamp down on us even harder, to the point of making it impossible for us to continue at all after the years of hard work and sacrifice we have put in, you need only keep consorting with representatives of the so-called freedom army—rebels, I brand them—and risk having word leak out about it."

Ersk sighed again. "I merely directed them toward a place they were already in search of. With or without me, they would have eventually gotten the same information from somewhere."

"Exactly. Eventually ... Somewhere ... From somewhere and somebody *else.* That's my point. You should have stayed out of it and *left it* to somebody else." Gretchel's narrowed eyes bored into her husband. "Besides, you did more than offer a few simple directions. You also lent them our servant boy to help guide the way to the mountain girl."

"I provided the *services* of Sandor. For a fee. A mighty handsome one, if I do say so myself."

"Go ahead and feel smug, you foolish man. I doubt the regulators would consider your handsome fee a distinction that mattered against the fact it came from aiding rebels." Gretchel folded her fleshy arm over a substantial bosom. "I, however, find that a bit of a saving grace ... Since you have rented out the services of our hired boy and thereby added to the work I will have to do in his absence, I think a healthy portion of the fee you received ought to be mine. I have long been depriving myself of any personal fineries in view of our financial straits. Therefore, particularly since the day has turned out fine and sunny for a trip to the village market, I think it is time and past time said deprivation came to an end ..."

III

Having finally been convinced that the words transcribed onto Nindocai's parchment were indeed a message from the goddess Arya (how else to account for the correlating revelations that fell into place too neatly to be mere coincidence?) Daer had pledged himself completely to the quest for the frozen treasure destined to finance the success of the freedom army. As had Spreek, who tended to follow faithfully wherever Daer led.

Bolstered by these additions, Nindocai and his already well-provisioned force had wasted no time striking north from the Boar's Tusk Inn. The arrangement for Sandor to accompany them was an added measure to help reach Serpentine Lake as expeditiously as possible. Inasmuch as none save the inn keeper and servant boy (not even Daer or Spreek) had ever heard of the place, trying to find it without a guide would have been both daunting and reckless, especially considering that the first breaths of winter could be expected in the high country in only a matter of weeks.

The inn keeper, Ersk, knew the way but could not personally guide them because he had grown too ponderously fat to make the trek. The route was too complicated to simply try and explain and Ersk's map drawing skills were too crude to attempt following with any degree of confidence. So it fell to Sandor then, who did not know the full way himself, to take them as far as a young woman named Pamella, a huntress for the same mountain tribe to which Sandor had belonged before his poor family indentured his services to Ersk and Gretchel. Pamella knew the high reaches and all its mysteries like no other and she was a cousin to Sandor, making the boy a perfect liaison to introduce Nindocai's group and help convince Pamella to lead them the rest of the way to that which they sought.

As they ascended out of the valley of Gahm, the remainder of their first day went well and their progress marked a good start. But all were keenly aware that the weather was bound to turn and the way ahead would only get more rugged.

With evening shadows lengthening and the sun sinking fast behind the westernmost peaks, the searchers halted and made camp for the night. A roll of stitched-together hides was unloaded from the pack horses and then unfurled and erected to form a tent-like shelter. A stone-ringed fire was soon crackling with warming flames. Grist and Lodor, veterans of the insurgency against the Wyvar invaders that had dragged on for so long, proved themselves skilled not only at waging battle but also at making a primitive camp as comfortable as possible. Under their direction, everyone pitched in as assigned (save for Nindocai, whose advanced years and priestly status earned him special consideration) and by nightfall their conditions were quite adequate. Once all had supped on thick mutton stew, coarse bread, and piping hot tea, it was agreed that Grist, Lodor, Daer, and Spreek would each take turns standing watch. The rest of the group and those not on duty were left to wrap themselves in their respective bedrolls and get some sleep.

* * *

That same night, back in the Gahm village, Rovark, captain of a twenty-man patrol of Wyvar regulators, sat at the rear table of a smoky grog shop consulting quietly but intently with his second in command. Rovark was a dark-featured man, lean and angular, with a sharp-pointed beard and a pale, crooked scar running from just below his left eye to the corner of his thin-lipped mouth. He emanated ruthless menace. His second, Kodan by name, was a brutish individual with a walrus mustache, massive shoulders, and huge, thick-fingered hands that looked as if they could crush rocks. Of the two, however, it was Rovark whose mere appearance struck a cold fear in the hearts of even stalwart men and whose presence was drawing nervous, sidelong glances from the other patrons in the grog shop this night.

"Nindocai," said Rovark, his lip curling as if saying the name left a bad taste in his mouth. "I remember hearing about him during my time down in the lowlands. A troublesome priest still clinging to his belief in the old gods of the Brassikans. Only a few days ago, there was a rumor circulating that he allegedly was on the move, trekking toward the highlands on some mysterious mission. It was hoped that at last he might be up to something that would be overt enough to seal his doom. From what I understand, special guard details were posted at numerous mountain passes to try and intercept him. But nothing came of it—either he was driven back by the weather of, with any luck, maybe the old rascal froze to death in his attempt to slip through. Everyone has known for years what he is, what he represents, yet no one could ever catch him in the act of holding a service or propagating his beliefs in any way."

"Why not simply crush the old troublemaker," grumbled Kodan. "Evidence against him could have been fabricated easily enough, it seems to me. That should have provided sufficient cause for taking action.

Rovark nodded. "Aye. That would have suited me, and surely the way we'd handle such a matter up here in our more isolated jurisdiction. But down in the lowlands there are too many prying eyes and too many of our own who cluck with the overly-cautious tongues of old women, reluctant to take any but the most unavoidable action for fear of further fanning the flames of the insurgency that continues to stubbornly smolder."

"The insurgency. Pah! The so-called 'freedom army'," Kodan sneered. "In my opinion, nothing more than rabble who poke and then run away like skittish girls in a schoolyard."

"Some play decidedly more roughly than schoolgirls," said the captain, absently touching a finger to the scar on his cheek. "But never mind that ... Tell me again about this woman who told you of Nindocai's presence here in our valley and the 'treasure quest' he allegedly is involved with."

"Her name is Gretchel, a sour-faced, sour-tempered waste of womanhood if ever I saw one," Kodan responded. "I overhead her talking with another woman in a pastry shop earlier this afternoon. Complaining, actually, is what she was doing ... something I wager she does with considerable frequency. About her husband most of the time, I further wager. The two of them run a little inn a bit farther up into the foot hills.

"Anyway, in this instance she was grousing about how her foolish husband had aided Nindocai and his party when they stopped over just last night, allegedly on their way to secure a treasure hidden in the frozen north. With the proceeds from this treasure, they openly stated their intent to finance the cause of the 'freedom army'. Overhearing the latter, of course, made me prick up my ears and take sharper note of the old cow's blabbering. Then I waited outside the pastry shop, grabbed her when she came out, dragged her into an alley and forced her to tell it to me all over again, making sure to spill every detail she knew."

"Do you believe she did?"

"Yes, I do. I had her whimpering and trembling to the point of practically wetting herself. Trust me, I put enough fear in her to make sure she wasn't holding anything back."

"I trust you also impressed upon her the importance of keeping better control over her loose tongue in the future—both in regard to the Nindocai business as well as her, ah, exchange with you?"

"Of course."

Rovark took a thoughtful sip of his grog. "Now the

question of what action we take based on her information. If she is right, Nindocai obviously made it past the guards at the mountain passes and now we know what it is he's up to."

Kodar looked puzzled for a moment before blurting, "It's the perfect opportunity to finally crush this troublesome priest, is it not? He's openly talking about seeking a way—whether this alleged frozen treasure truly exists or not—to help the insurgents, the ridiculously named 'freedom army'. That's blatant treason and justification for the harshest of actions."

"No doubt about what needs to be done where Nindocai is concerned. We strike out after him and his traitorous group first thing in the morning," Rovark agreed. "But what comes once we've dealt with them … What if the treasure *does* exist?"

* * *

Due to Ersk's tremendous girth (which was hardly to say that his wife herself was slight of build) it had been many years since the couple had shared the same bed in their quarters at the rear of the Boar's Tusk Inn. On this night, that was a particularly fortunate thing for Gretchel. Had it been otherwise, the restless tossing and turning that refused to allow her sleep surely would have been questioned by her mate.

As it was, she only had herself to answer to and that was proving bothersome enough.

Ever since that dreadful, bullying regulator Kodan had cornered her in the village and threatened her into revealing everything she'd overheard regarding

Nindocai and the others, Gretchel had been a nervous, guilt-ridden wreck.

The guilt came from having to face the undeniable fact that her revelations had betrayed those working in the interest of freeing her country from the hated Wyvar invaders. No matter how preposterous she thought the talk of a "frozen treasure" was or how futile she outwardly claimed the rebel efforts to be, she nevertheless harbored a measure of hope that someday, somehow they might succeed. Certainly she did not want to be responsible for the failure of what might an important mission. Above all, she was sickened by the thought that fatalities within Nindocai's group might occur as a result of the things she'd said.

The agony within herself over such a possibility was bad enough. But her anxieties at the thought of Ersk finding out was even worse. No matter the shoddy treatment and frequent verbal abuse she directed toward her husband, in her own way Gretchel actually loved him a great deal. And she believed he must love her, too. Why else would he put up with the way she treated him? But she also knew how strongly he felt about his beloved Brassik and how fervently he wanted the insurgency to succeed. Did he love her enough to forgive her if he ever found out about her betrayal, inadvertent and partially forced though it had been?

Years had passed since Gretchel last prayed to any of the old gods. Even before the Wyvars came and forbade it, she had not been an overly religious person. But tonight she desperately felt the need to appeal to a higher power.

Wasn't Nindocai supposed to be a priest directly linked to Arya—the goddess of Hope? That's certainly what she could use now, Gretchel told herself. Hope. Hope that her careless tongue did not result in causing all the damage she feared ... And further hope that she had learned from this misery and would speak more wisely and discreetly in the future.

IV

For two more days Nindocai's group forged northward.

The day following their first night's encampment was again relatively mild until late in the afternoon when the temperature dropped rapidly and a heightened bitter wind whistled in out of the west. As before, however, Grist and Lodor saw to it that their night camp was made reasonably comfortable.

But the cold and the wind continued throughout the next morning. This, in conjunction with the path of their ascent up into the higher mountainous reaches growing steadily more rugged, made for slower, harder progress. Although he issued no complaint, everyone could see that this was particularly taxing on the aged Nindocai.

Their mid-afternoon arrival at the cave dwellings occupied by the tribe of Sandor and Pamella, the huntress they'd come in search of, was a relief to all. Recognizing a member of their own leading the visitors, the tribe elders signaled not only a hearty welcome to the group but an evening celebration was also promptly arranged. Having young Sandor reunited with his parents—though only temporarily, it was understood, inasmuch as he would eventually have to return to the Boar's Tusk Inn to fulfill the obligation of his indenturement—added a nice bonus to the proceedings.

Feasting on goat and mountain boar, garnished with root and berry preservatives, while being entertained by dancers leaping and gyrating to the beat of hollowed stone drums, Nindocai and Daer conferred with the tribe elders on the full details of their mission. Although the ravages of the Wyvar overthrow had only very indirectly touched this primitive place, the elders had a good awareness of what had transpired down on the lowlands and were supportive of driving out the invaders. In view of this—with the provisos that the huntress in question was willing and that she'd be allowed to return in time to resume her duties for the sake of helping keep the tribe supplied with meat to last through the heart of winter—they were amenable to Pamella serving as their guide.

It wasn't until the festivities were winding down that Pamella herself put in an appearance. And quite a striking entrance she made—striding tall and statuesque and stunning through the swirling smoke and flickering firelight of the cavern. She came to a halt and stood directly in front of where the elders and the visitors sat sipping post meal spiced tea. Her sloe-eyed gaze passed across the faces and hulking shapes of Grist, Lodor, and Daer (lingering on the latter a barely discernible beat longer than on the others?) before coming to rest on Nindocai.

"Are you the holy man who asks for me by name? Seeking my services, I am told, to guide you to Serpentine Lake?"

"If you are the huntress Pamella," answered the priest, "then, yes, you have been told correctly."

"I am indeed her," answered the bold young woman, proudly tossing her mane of copper hair.

"The final decision is yours, of course," spoke up the head elder. "But we believe the mission of these men to be a just one. You have our blessing to aid them if you wish."

Pamella's gaze once again swept over the strangers before her and then, once again, came to rest on Nindocai. "In that case, what are my services worth to you?" she asked bluntly.

Nindocai took a moment to consider her question before replying. "We are not men of any appreciable wealth, if that is what you are asking. What resources we *were* able to call upon went into the outfitting of our group. In complete candor, however ... as has already been explained to your tribal council ... what we are seeking is an alleged treasure that we believe to be of considerable wealth. In the event we are successful in finding same, then we naturally would be willing to reward you handsomely."

Pamella's mouth twisted wryly. "Spoken like a true lowlander, holy man or otherwise." She made a gesture with one hand. "Look around you. Do either I or my people look like monetary gain is the driving goal in our lives? We are simple folk who live here, the way we do, because we shun the greed and deceit and corruption of the lowland ways. The mountains give us everything we need, as long as we have the weapons and tools and other basics to survive in them ... Occasional purchases of such items, to augment that which we fashion for ourselves, are the only use we ever have for the precious money so many of your kind worship more highly than any god."

"That is an admirable sentiment," agreed Nindocai. "I, too, have a healthy disdain for money and the many evils attached to it. But there are instances, as even you admit, where it is necessary. Our purpose in searching for the treasure I mentioned is only for the cause of furnishing our freedom army for *their* basic needs in order to one day drive back the Wyvar hordes which overran our nation so many cursed months and years ago."

A flicker of compassion came and went on Pamella's strong-featured face.

Daer stood up. "I am Daer," he introduced himself. "Pardon my immodestly, but I am widely considered one of the best blacksmiths in all of Brassik. I make the finest arrowheads, bladed weapons, plow shares, or any other type of forged instrument you can name. Items that can make your survival in—aye, even conquest of—these mountains far easier than you've ever experienced. Let's negotiate a quantity of these kinds of items that you think your services may be worth. We'll reach an agreement and then, when we've returned from our quest, I will provide you with whatever we settle on."

Pamella regarded him intently but did not respond right away. Then: "At least you understand the kind of currency that is meaningful to me and mine. But how can I be sure that you are a man of your word or that the quality of your work is as lofty as your own opinion of it?"

From a shadowy patch just back from one of the cave's fire pits, where he sat with his family members, Sandor spoke up. "I can vouch for Daer being a man of the highest integrity, cousin. And the only thing that matches the quality of his word is the quality of his work."

Still looking at Daer, Pamella arched a single eyebrow. "You certainly have impressed one member of our tribe, blacksmith."

"If you want further verification of at least part of what the boy claims," said Lodor, stepping forward and holding out his precisely balanced combat spear with its gleaming steel tip, "you need look no further than this as an example of Daer's craftsmanship."

"Nor this," added Grist, holding out one of his steel-tipped arrows.

Pamella took the items and examined them. Her eyes quickly shone with recognition and appreciation for their quality.

Handing back the items, the huntress fixed her gaze once again on Daer. "Your point has been convincingly made," she said. "Let us commence negotiating quantities and reach an agreement quickly ... Everyone will want to turn in as soon as possible, for we'll be starting out in the morning before dawn."

V

"There it lies," said Pamella, pointing, as the others closed around her. "This peak is one of the few vantage points from which one can see the lake's full length and all the twists and turns that gives it its name."

Several hundred yards below the rocky crest where they stood gathered, the frozen surface of Serpentine Lake stretched out between snow-crusted slopes broken by thick stands of pine and taller oak and ash trees with denuded branches poking up like empty hands with gnarled fingers reaching toward the leaden sky. At the far end of the lake, where it flared and then narrowed again, wedge-like, a wall of sheer ice rose up into a blurring mist.

"In the distance is the Dragon Glacier," added Pamella, as if to remove any doubt. "Legend has it that the name comes from a once fierce volcano that burnt itself out and then was swallowed by the ice."

"The frozen fire beast, in accordance with Arya's words," murmured Nindocai. "It is there then, at the wall of ice, where I believe we will find the treasure."

Not quite under his breath, Spreek muttered sourly, "What a treat. After days of clambering up and down these icy mountains, now we get to skim across a frozen lake so we can go hug a glacier."

"Bite your constantly complaining tongue," Daer snapped at him. "If Arya's treasure awaits us here, then the trifling hardships we've endured to make it this far will amount to little if they result in our being able to hand over the means for victory to our freedom army."

It was near the close of the fifth day since their departure from the warm caves of Pamella's tribe. And, true to Spreek's lament, no portion of the way had been easy. In addition to the rugged terrain, the weather had presented little but cold rain, flurries of snow, and constant battering winds. Only the unerring course set by Pamella and her equally unerring accuracy with her bow to keep them in fresh meat, combined with the camp-making skills of Grist and Lodor, had made it bearable at all.

Despite the toll these conditions clearly took on the frail and aged priest, Nindocai forged on without complaint. And Spreek, who groused and grumbled at every opportunity, nevertheless proved—despite his bellyaching and physical shortcomings—that he could be counted on for any task required of him. As was the case with all members of the party, including the two youths, Ryle and Sandor, who formed a solid friendship along the way.

And now the prize they sought—if the words of the goddess had been interpreted correctly—was at hand.

"We should descend down into the tree line and make our night camp there, where we'll have fuel and a good wind block," suggested Pamella. "In the morning, the descent the rest of the way to the lake will be relatively easy. And once on the frozen surface, the going will be smooth and level all the way to the glacier. We should reach it by mid-day."

None found fault with the huntress's suggestion and so they followed it until they reached a suitable spot to begin pitching camp.

* * *

A quarter league away, on the back trail of Nindocai's party, Captain Rovark had climbed down from his saddle and now sat on the slanted trunk of a fallen tree where he listened intently to the report being turned in by his lead scout. "So at last they've led us to the mysterious lake," Rovark grunted with weary satisfaction when the scout had finished his telling.

Standing nearby, his broad face set in a grim expression, Kodan spoke in a somber tone. "And not a minute too soon. This hateful terrain and its blasted weather conditions have taken a worrisome toll on our men. I don't know how much more they could take without an end in sight."

Rovark thrust to his feet, face contorting with anger, "And I don't know how much more I can take of their whining and sniveling! They're supposed to be fighting men, are they not? That means fighting and conquering whatever foe—be it someone wielding a sword or hard conditions and bad weather—they're called upon to face. Is that so difficult to comprehend?"

"No, sir. It's not," said Kodan, frowning. "It's just that …"

"Just that what?"

"Well, they're much better trained and prepared for

fighting than for clambering over half-frozen rocks for hours and days without once drawing their swords or the strings of their bows. They're anxious for the chance to do that, and they don't understand why we haven't long since attacked these rebels instead of just following along behind."

Scowling, Rovark motioned away the scout who had given his report. When the man was gone, the captain turned his attention back to Kodan and said in a lowered tone, "I have my reasons and you alone know what they are. I didn't embark on this undertaking merely to spill another splash of rebel blood. I want more than that. I want the treasure that awaits the Brassik dogs at the end of their quest. Once I am certain they have it in their grasp and that there is no final bit of secrecy or trickery to keep it from falling into ours … Then I will have their damn blood *and* their treasure!"

VI

Exactly as Pamella had predicted, the middle of the following day found Nindocai and his party standing at the base of the massive ice wall. As if signaling some kind of good omen, the morning had dawned clear and bright with no trace of the knifing wind that had been cutting into them for days.

Once the relief and awe of making it this far had been allowed to sink in, however, there still remained the task of actually finding the treasure. In order to do this, the group split up and fanned out to begin exploring the shorelines on either of side of the narrowed lake surface where the wedge-shaped head of the "serpent" thrust into the glacier. This shoreline consisted primarily of staggered ledges of lava rock choked with brushy pine growth. These jagged ledges had to be scaled in numerous places and then the pine bushes pushed through to gain access to the glacial ice behind. The breadth of the ice wall, spreading much wider than the point of the lake itself, made the climbing and bush-beating a somewhat painstaking and time-consuming chore.

In the end, it was Spreek the Scrounger who spotted what appeared to be the prize they had come in search of. His eager shout brought the others scrambling to congregate around him.

"There," he said breathlessly, gesturing to a section of the ice wall just above the surface of the ledge he'd crawled to and cleared and where they now all stood. It took a minute for the others to focus on what the sharp eyes of the little man had spied. But then, gradually, through the murkiness of the ice, they all saw it … a shapeless, softly glittering yellowish mass wrapped in the embrace of *the frozen fire beast*.

"Great Critt Almighty," whispered Nindocai reverently. "It truly exists and is within our grasp … Praise be to the Goddess of Hope, we have succeeded!"

"But how will we get it out of there?" asked Lodor. "I can't judge for certain, but it appears buried pretty far back in the ice."

"We brought ice axes, did we not? They're on the pack horses," said Daer.

"True enough," agreed Grist. He gestured to Ryle and Sandor. "You two lads go fetch the horses over here closer, we'll need them to load the treasure on anyway." He drew his sword. "In the meantime, Lodor and I will make this clearing a bit wider for us to work within."

"You may go ahead and widen the clearing," said Nindocai. "But I don't believe the ice axes will be necessary."

Daer frowned. "Why do you say that, holy one?"

Nindocai smiled faintly as he tipped his head to indicate the hammer that Daer carried, slipped through his thick leather belt. "You're forgetting part of your destiny, Daer. Your hammer … Use *it* on the ice."

Everyone looked on with expressions of

uncertainty.

Daer hesitated. "Are you sure?"

Nindocai tipped his head again, in a single nod. "I am."

Daer stepped up to where the golden mass shown vaguely through the ice. He pulled the hammer from his belt, rolled his thick shoulders. Then he drew back the hammer and swung it forward with all his might, crashing the work-scarred head hard against the ice.

The ice dented deeply under the impact and sparkling shards spat away. But, for a long moment, nothing more happened. Daer straightened up and appeared somewhat disconcerted.

And then there was a shockingly loud *craaack!* of sound. A spiderweb of fissures began spreading away from the indentation of the hammer strike. All gathered on the ledge took a step backward. The spiderweb quickly spread to a width and height of nearly six feet until it suddenly collapsed into a thousand crunching, tinkling ice chips that rained down to form a slushy pile.

Beyond, a large cavity had been exposed. A soft illumination filled this opening and from it emanated a curious warmth. And in the heart of this cavity sat a huge chest filled to overflowing with coins, bracelets, goblets, and various other trinkets, all of solid gold.

For a long time no one spoke. They all stood in stunned silence, gazing into the just-revealed chamber and its amazing contents.

It was Spreek who broke the silence, saying in a hushed voice, "Daer, you've done some fine work with your hammer before ... but never anything close to equaling this."

* * *

The group's euphoria at uncovering the treasure and thus succeeding in their mission was so great that the task of hauling the treasure down out of the chamber seemed like child's play. Daer, Spreek, and Sandor transferred the contents of the chest into the sturdy leather saddlebags they'd brought along for that very purpose; these were handed down to Grist, Lodor, and Ryle, who had brought the pack animals up onto the shoreline as far as even the sure-footed beasts dared go, and there began loading the saddlebags onto them.

While this was taking place, Nindocai busied himself examining the interior of the hollow treasure chamber. He was fascinated by the warmth it held and the source of its soft illumination. Both of these seemed to come from its back wall, an area of the chamber where the ice surface had a peculiar glazed-over quality.

Outside the chamber, a restless Pamella prowled back and forth, closely scanning the surrounding lava ridges and the empty lake that now stretched behind them as she paced.

"You seem troubled," observed Daer, pausing momentarily in his work. "Is there something wrong?"

The huntress frowned. "I'm not sure. I ... I sense something. Like there are eyes upon us. Someone watching."

"Isn't that rather unlikely?"

"It should be, of course. But I had the same feeling a time or two on the journey here ... Only never this strong."

Daer paused a moment longer, his own gaze sweeping over the area. "There's an unnerving feel to this place, no denying that. But we'll be finished here soon and then be on our way back home."

"I will welcome that."

No sooner were these words spoken than the source of Pamella's instinctive concerns was revealed. From the lava ridges and undergrowth across the narrowed point of the lake streaked a volley of blood-hungry war arrows. First there was the escalating hum of these missiles in flight and then, a micro-instant later, their savage tips began striking. Lodor and Grist fell almost immediately, each taking more than one fatal hit. More arrows came. The pack horses were dropped with a heavy concentration and young Ryle, only grazed, had the intelligence to fall behind one of them for cover. On the slightly higher ledge at the mouth of the treasure chamber, Daer took a piercing wound to his shoulder that caused him to fall back through the opening. Pamella ducked in after him as more arrows rattled harmlessly against ice and rock surfaces on all sides.

As suddenly as it had started, the attack halted.

An abrupt silence gripped the scene across the great ice wall's base.

Inside the treasure chamber, Nindocai and Pamella rushed to aid the wounded Daer. They wasted no time pulling the arrow from him and quickly stanching the flow of blood from the wound. Loyal Spreek hovered close by with frantic concern.

"Critt's Thunder!" exclaimed the blacksmith.

"What happened? What in blazes is going on?"

Before anyone inside the chamber could attempt an answer, a harsh voice called from across the narrow point of the frozen lake.

"Holy man Nindocai!" said Captain Rovark. "Can you hear me? I know you and the others are inside the ice cave. We've killed your rebel fighters, your guardians. If you want to be given any chance for the rest of you to survive, you'd better talk to me and beg for your lives."

Nindocai moved to the edge of the chamber's opening and called back. "I will never beg to murdering heathen dogs!"

"Then you are certain to die. You and all the remainder of your foolish followers ... unless you think the old gods you so stubbornly cling to will work some kind of miracle to save you."

"Who are you?" Nindocai demanded.

"I am Captain Rovark of the Wyvar Regulators."

"Then my gods have already worked a miracle by bringing me here to unearth the treasure that will finance the freedom army for its victory over you and your whole heathen horde!"

Rovark's mocking laughter rang out. "Are you as blind as you are foolish? The treasure is no longer yours. Your fighters and your pack animals are dead. You are defeated and at my mercy. The gold you have unearthed is going nowhere—except to *me*!"

Pamella darted to the opening for the split second it took to fit an arrow to her bow and send it streaking in the direction of Rovark's voice. "Not all of our fighters are dead, Wyvar cur," she shouted before ducking back to cover. "Step out and face me! Send you cowardly archers and I will gladly trade arrows with them. We will see who ends up at who's mercy!"

Again Rovark's mocking laughter. "Ah, the huntress is as feisty as she is lovely. I'm glad she is still alive. Not that I'd hesitate to kill her if I have to. But, taken alive, I can envision ways she would surely sweeten my treasure haul."

"You are a cur *and* a disgusting pig!" Pamella shouted back. "I'd sooner slit my throat than be taken alive and succumb to your debauchery."

"Those are brave words, my feisty one. Soon we will see how willing you are to truly back them up. And the same for your archery challenge. You see, we've been following you for days and have noted the mere handful of arrows in your quiver … Even if you strike true with every shot you take, you haven't the ammunition to put down all of my men."

Pamella retreated deeper into the treasure chamber. Her bosom rising and falling rapidly, she said, "I think they're getting ready to attack. And the captain is right—I have just a limited number of arrows and my bow is the only long range weapon we have to repel them."

"If they come," said Daer gruffly, "I'll drop down to where Lodor and Grist fell. I'll seize up one of their swords and, even with my injury, I swear some attackers will pay with their lives before I go down all the way."

Nindocai shook his head. "There may not be a need

for that, Daer. There may be a better way."

The blacksmith frowned. "This is no time to be speaking in riddles, holy man. If you have something to say, say it!"

"Very well. Let me start by saying that my faith refuses to allow me to believe that the goddess Arya led us here only to see us fall victims to this Wyvar scum. Trust me, she has provided a means for our salvation and I believe I know what it is."

"Then what are you waiting for? Now would seem like a very good time to share it with the rest of us."

Turning instead to Spreek, Nindocai told him, "Go watch the opening. Take care not to target yourself. Let us know when the regulators start across."

The master scrounger did as instructed, squirming his diminutive and twisted shape into a notch in the slush that had initially fallen from Daer's hammer strike. Over his shoulder, he said, "They're not doing anything yet. And I can see Ryle down below, he's motioning that he is okay."

"Good. Indicate for him to stay put and stay low," Nindocai responded.

Then, turning back to Daer and Pamella, the holy man motioned for them to follow him deeper into the chamber, to the rear wall with its glazed-over appearance and soft, heat-emanating glow. "Just beyond this," he said, "I believe that the dragon for which this glacier was named still lives and breathes. It is he who will aid us in the defeat of Rovark and his bloodletters."

"More riddles," spat Daer. "I grow tired of this, old

man."

The warning from Spreek suddenly rang out. "Here they come! They're swarming full force across the narrow part of the lake!"

A sudden intensity flared in Nindocai's eyes. This he fixed full on Daer. "If your faith in Arya is real, you must call upon it now. You must trust in it and in me." Again the holy man pointed. "It's up to you, Daer—you and your mighty hammer. Strike once more. Strike the glowing wall!"

After a moment of tense hesitation, strike Daer did. He drew back his good arm and swung it forward with all his strength—this time crashing his hammer against the glazed, eerily glowing wall.

As before, there was at first a pause with no evident result. And then a sound began to build. Not a startling *crack!* like before, but now a low growl that slowly, steadily built in volume until it became a rolling, rumbling roar. Nor was there a spider web spreading outward from the impact point of the hammer strike this time. Rather, through the glowing, opaque glaze, Daer could see a pronged fissure squirming inward from his blow, reaching deeper into the ice until it disappeared.

And then, as the roaring sound reached a near ear-splitting crescendo, the floor of the chamber began to shake. The lava ridges on all sides trembled and started to crumble. Huge shards broke away from the shivering, splitting ice wall and hurtled down like frozen lightning bolts, stabbing into the icy surface of the lake that was already breaking apart on its own. The charging regulators were caught in mid attack, unable to turn and retreat in time before they were either crushed by giant icicles from above or plunged through the splitting ice beneath their feet to a drowning death in the foaming, numbingly cold exposed water.

The culmination of this chaotic upheaval was the release of a single great lava spew from behind the quaking but still-holding ice wall, arcing high into the air amid a sulfurous black plume and then pouring down onto what had been a solidly frozen lake surface only moments earlier, resulting in the release of a tumbling, hissing monster cloud of steam that rolled outward and filled the whole valley.

The ledges on either side of the narrowed V of water held for the most part, in spite of much trembling and crumbling. Those in and about the treasure cave were relatively unscathed save for being badly shaken up and mildly singed by the roiling steam.

Gradually, the ground stopped trembling and the roaring hiss of the steam grew quiet.

A heavy fog settled in and gave no indication of dissipating any time soon, Sandor and Spreek slipped down to the ledge where Ryle was and assisted him in crawling up to join them and the others in the cocoon-like safety of the former treasure chamber.

They all huddled there together and remained that way into the night.

At some point, in the pervasive quiet, Daer asked, "How could you know, Nindocai, that a second hammer blow by me would have that result?"

The holy man smiled thinly. "I didn't. Not exactly. But my examination of this chamber's back wall, its strange glow and warmth, told me that the supposedly dormant volcano must still have a pocket of life left in it. Additionally, as I said earlier, I couldn't bring myself to believe that Arya had urged us here only to fall victim to Wyvar butchery—or to the hellfire of the volcano. So I put my faith in Her and in your marvelous hammer, Daer, and … well, you know the rest."

"Poor Lodor and Grist. They never had a chance," said Ryle sadly.

"But we still have the gold they died for," Nindocai pointed out. "The treasure that will finance the freedom army and help defeat the Wyvar invaders. They would have gladly sacrificed themselves for that."

"The only trouble is," Pamella reminded everyone, "we no longer have pack animals to transport the gold. Our horses also fell to the regulator arrows."

"We can walk out and get more horses if we have to," Daer said stubbornly.

"That may not be necessary," said Spreek. "From what I saw, the regulators were charging across the ice on foot. They left their horses in the lava ridges on the other side. Seems likely most of them would have survived the volcano eruption, just as we did on this side. If the lake sufficiently freezes over again by morning, we should be able to go over there and catch enough of them to use for new pack animals."

"If need be, we can go around the far end of the lake and come back to catch them," said Daer.

"Maybe," allowed Spreek. And then, cocking one eyebrow sharply above his wizened face, he added, "But if we *do* go across the ice, Daer, just do me a favor and leave that hammer of yours on this side."

Daer looked puzzled. "Why is that?"

"Because," Spreek explained, "I don't want to be out on the ice with you in case the hammer accidently slips and falls from your belt … there's no telling what will happen next if that thing hits the ice again."

Daer continued to look puzzled for a moment. And then, abruptly, his face split with a wide grin and he began to laugh—a hearty, booming, tension-easing laugh that was joined in by all the others until it rolled out and floated over the scene for a long, welcome time.

†

ABOUT THE AUTHOR

WAYNE D. DUNDEE lives in the once-notorious old cowtown of Ogallala, on the hinge of Nebraska's panhandle. A widower, retired from a managerial position in the magnetics industry, Dundee now devotes full time to his writing.

To date, Dundee has had nearly a score of novels and novellas plus over thirty short stories published. Much of his work has featured his PI protagonist, Joe Hannibal (celebrating over thirty years on the fictional detective scene and appearing most recently in Blade of the Tiger, 2013). He also dabbles in fantasy and straight crime, and lately has done some notable work in the Western genre. His 2010 Western short story, "This Old Star," won a Peacemaker Award from the Western Fictioneers writers' organization. His 2011 novel Dismal River won a Peacemaker in the Best First Western Novel category. His 2012 story "Adeline" won a third Peacemaker, again in the short story category.

Titles in the Hannibal series have been translated into several languages and nominated for an Edgar, an Anthony, and six Shamus Awards. Dundee is also the founder and original editor of *Hardboiled Magazine*.

ALSO BY WAYNE D. DUNDEE
FROM BEAT TO A PULP BOOKS

From the Cash Laramie and Gideon Miles series

MANHUNTER'S MOUNTAIN — Manhunter's Mountain shows a powerful side to Cash Laramie as he makes his way down the side of a mountain with a prisoner in tow, and two prostitutes eager to flee a mining town that's gone bust, looking to make a new life for themselves. An early winter storm promises to make the journey more than a normal struggle. And, leaving town with two of its most precious gems, the prostitutes, puts Cash in the crosshairs of an angry gang of men who are willing to keep the women in town ... at any cost.

THE GUNS OF VEDAUWOO — U.S. Marshal Cash Laramie is sent out to locate a shipment of stolen guns in the Vedauwoo area of Wyoming where the rocky terrain is treacherous and enshrouded in mystical beauty. In his quest, Cash goes up against an amoral opportunist looking to stir up discord in the region by selling the weapons to a group of Native Americans.

THE EMPTY BADGE — It's been weeks since Cash Laramie, the famed "Outlaw Marshal," has been heard from. Meanwhile, at the Federal Marshal headquarters in Cheyenne, Wyoming, some disturbing reports are starting to filter in about the notorious Driscoll Gang rapidly hitting a series of banks, allegedly with the aid of a badge-wearing accomplice claiming to be Laramie. Can it be true? Can it be that the lawman with the hair-trigger temper and the mile-wide independent streak has finally gone completely rogue?

From the Drifter Detective series

WIDE SPOT IN THE ROAD

Jack Laramie, grandson of the legendary U.S. Marshal Cash Laramie, is a tough-as-nails WWII vet roaming the modern West. He lives out of a horse trailer hitched to the back of a DeSoto, searching out P.I. gigs to keep him afloat.

Jack stops in the remote town of Buele's Corner for a bite to eat. Before he finishes his bowl of chili, he gets caught up in a tornado of events that starts with a panicked, young couple racing into the diner to use the phone to call for help—a menacing motorcycle gang, The Deguelloes, is chasing after them. When the couple discovers the phone is out of order, Jack steps in to help them fend off the gang who's accusing the couple of running some of their fellow bikers off the road.

From The Lawyer series

STAY OF EXECUTION — In the Old West, J.D. Miller had been an attorney at law. A respected and successful one. Until the horrific, soul-scarring day when he returned home to find his entire family slaughtered—the charred remains scarcely recognizable in the smoldering ruins of what had once been their house. Like a phoenix rising out of the ashes, The Lawyer—a killing machine—was born, and he's leaving a blood-splattered revenge trail as he searches out those who murdered his family.

THE RETRIBUTIONERS — J.D. Miller, aka The Lawyer, continues to hunt the men that slaughtered his family. His next target is Jules Despare who's been riding with the Selkirk gang robbing banks. When the town of Emmett, Texas, is marked by the hardcases and the local marshal murdered, The Lawyer is asked by the town's influential residents to track down the reprehensible outfit. But he has little use for the narrow-minded bigots that won't stand behind the remaining deputy—a black man named Ernest Tell. After Tell resigns, he suggests a partnership with The Lawyer who refuses. It's obvious, though, these two avengers are gunning for the same men and will eventually work together to settle old scores.

Offering short story collections and novellas in a variety of genres (from noir and hardboiled crime to Westerns, from science fiction to the undefinable), BEAT to a PULP is sure to have something for every pulp enthusiast. See what's new in our catalog from some of the finest pulp writers of today

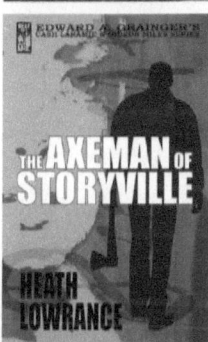